MARY

Specially
Sarah

Illustrated by Joanna Carey

MAMMOTH

For all my daughters,
but specially Sarah

First published in Great Britain 1987
by Methuen Children's Books Ltd
Magnet paperback edition first published 1988
Published 1991 by Mammoth
an imprint of Mandarin Paperbacks
Michelin House, 81 Fulham Road, London SW3 6RB

Mandarin is an imprint of the Octopus Publishing Group,
a division of Reed International Books Ltd

Text copyright © 1987 Mary Hoffman
Illustrations copyright © 1987 Joanna Carey

ISBN 0 7497 1204 X

A CIP catalogue record for this title
is available from the British Library

Printed in Great Britain
by Cox & Wyman Ltd, Reading, Berkshire

Specially
Sarah

Sarah lives with her family in a house
with a red door. She now goes to school
all day, but secretly wishes she could
come home at dinner-time and eat her
lunch with Mummy, Nana and her cat
Jam Samwidge.

Also by Mary Hoffman

All About Lucy
Just Jack

for younger readers

Nancy No-Size

Contents

ONE

Sarah and the Birthday Party

Sarah lived with her family in a house with a red door. Her family was her mother and her father and her Nana and her little sister Lucy and her marmalade cat, Jam Samwidge. Lucy was too little to go to proper school so she went to nursery. Sarah used to go to the same nursery when she was little, but now she was in the infants. She stayed at school all day, but she often wished she could come home at dinner-time like Lucy and eat her lunch with Mummy and Nana.

One day, Sarah came home from school with an invitation. It said: "Please come to Kathy's party on Sunday afternoon."

Mummy said, "Isn't that nice?"

Sarah said, "I don't want to go to Kathy's party."

Her mummy was very surprised. "But there

will be lots of party games – musical chairs and
pass-the-parcel and blind-man's buff. I'm sure
you'll have a lovely time."

Her daddy said, "There'll be lots of food too,
I bet. Ice-cream and jelly and sausages on
sticks and birthday cake and chocolate
biscuits. It makes me feel hungry just to think

8

of it. What's for tea?"

Sarah said, "I don't like jelly."

Her Nana said, "You can wrap up a present for Kathy and give her a card. You can come shopping with me to choose it if you like."

Sarah shook her head.

Lucy said, "If Sarah doesn't want to go, can I go instead? I could wear my pink party dress."

But all Sarah would say was, "I don't want to go."

On Saturday, Sarah's mummy said, "All your best friends from your class are going to Kathy's party, you know. Jamie, Nicola and Natasha and Benjamin and David. You'll be the odd one out if you don't go. Won't you change your mind?"

But Sarah said, "No."

On Saturday morning, Sarah woke up with a horrible cold.

"Oh dear," said her mummy, "now you won't be able to go to Kathy's party. What a shame!"

"Atishoo!" said Sarah.

Sarah's mummy rang Kathy's mummy and said, "I'm so sorry, but Sarah can't come to the party. She's got a horrible cold." Sarah's daddy wrapped up Kathy's present and took it round to her house. (It was a frog that squirts

9

water out of its mouth when you squeeze it in the bath.) Sarah stayed in bed all day.

When she was well enough to go back to school, Sarah heard all about the party. The children had played musical chairs and pass-the-parcel and blind-man's buff. They had had birthday cake to eat and ice-cream and jelly and lots of chocolate biscuits. They had all got very sticky and grubby and had to be washed before they went home. Everyone said it had been a *very good* party.

A week later, Sarah got another invitation. It said: "Please come to Nicola and Natasha's birthday party next Saturday."

"Hmm," said Sarah's mummy.

"Well?" said her daddy.

"I could make you a new dress," said her Nana.

"All right," said Sarah, "I'll go."

"Can I share what's in your party bag?" asked Lucy.

Next Saturday, Sarah did go to Nicola and Natasha's party. Kathy was there and so were Benjamin and David and Jamie. They all played musical chairs, pass-the-parcel and blind-man's buff. They had ice-cream and jelly and chocolate biscuits and *two* birthday cakes because Nicola and Natasha were twins. At six o'clock Sarah's mother and father came to collect her. Mummy gave her a big hug and asked if she had had a nice time.

"Ye-s," said Sarah. "The party was good but I got a bit frightened near the end."

"Why?" asked Daddy. "Did something nasty happen?"

"No," said Sarah, snuggling into Mummy's coat, "but I thought you might forget to collect me. And then I'd have to stay at Nicola and Natasha's house for ever."

"Never!" said Daddy. "We couldn't do without a Sarah at our house."

Next month it was Sarah's own birthday.

"Do you want a party?" asked her mummy, "or don't you like parties?"

"Oh, please have one," said Lucy. "I *can* come to that one, can't I?"

"Of course I want a party," said Sarah. She invited Kathy and Benjamin and David and Nicola and Natasha and Jamie.

She told her mummy and daddy all the things she wanted to eat and the games she wanted to play. She wore the dress that Nana had made her for the twins' party and Lucy wore her pink one.

When the children came they all played musical chairs and pass-the-parcel and blind-man's buff. Lucy joined in all the games but she got some of them a bit wrong. Jam Samwidge joined in too but he got them even more wrong. Sarah was a bit sad that she didn't win pass-the-parcel, because the prize was a very

12

nice helicopter she had chosen herself. But she cheered up when Jam Samwidge helped them play a game that Nana had invented which involved rolling up balls of wool to find what was tied to the other end.

Then they had a wonderful birthday tea, with sausages on sticks and crisps and biscuits and ice-cream (without jelly) and a big birthday cake in the shape of a hedgehog, which Sarah's mummy had made. The candles looked like extra spikes and when Sarah blew them out they all lit up again, so everyone had a go at blowing them out.

At the end of the party all the children were collected by their mummies and daddies. No-one was left behind except Sarah and Lucy and that was all right because they were home already. Sarah's mummy flopped down into an armchair and kicked off her shoes. Jam Samwidge cleaned up all the bits of sausage from under the table.

"Phew, what an afternoon!" said Sarah's daddy, who had been organising the games.

"I'll put the kettle on," said Nana.

"Do you like parties now, Sarah?" said Lucy.

"Yes," said Sarah. "Especially when they happen here. I wish *everyone* could have their

13

birthday parties at our house!"

TWO

Sarah
and the
Red Things

"What can I have that's red?" asked Sarah one day at tea-time. "Miss Munro wants us all to bring things to school for our Red Table."

"How about a strawberry?" said Nana, who was spreading jam on some toast.

"It's the wrong time of the year for strawberries," said Sarah's mummy.

"Someone would eat it anyway," said Lucy, who was very fond of strawberries.

"What about your red socks?" suggested Sarah's daddy.

"No," said Sarah, "Miss Munro can't have those, because I want to wear them tomorrow, with the tartan skirt Nana gave me for my birthday."

"It should be very easy to find something that's red," said Mummy, "because red is Sarah's favourite colour. There's your pillar-box money-box, for instance."

"No good," said Sarah. "I need it to put my pocket money in because I'm saving up for a helicopter."

"I know," said Lucy, picking up the cat. "You can take Jam Samwidge."

The car purred.

"He's not red," said Sarah, stroking him behind the ears. "He's orange. Besides, he's not allowed on tables!"

"Let's all close our eyes and think of all the red things we can," said Daddy.

"All right," said Sarah, closing her eyes. "Jam tarts, traffic lights, my toothbrush and big London buses."

"Newborn babies, clown's noses, sunsets and our front door," said Mummy.

"Uncle Thomas's hair, Nana's car, chilli peppers and Irish Setters," said Daddy.

"Red Riding Hood's hood, ketchup, ladybirds and Father Christmas," said Lucy.

"Fire engines, my winter nightie, danger signs and Sarah's wellingtons," said Nana.

They all opened their eyes.

"That's it," said Mummy. "She can take the wellingtons for the Red Table."

"But I'm sure it's going to rain tomorrow," said Sarah. "and if it does I want to *wear* my

16

wellingtons."

"What are we to do?" said Daddy. "Most of the red things we can think of are not the sort you can take to school, like our front door. And all the red things we *could* take are things that Sarah specially likes because red is her favourite colour."

After tea, Sarah and Lucy went all round the house looking for red things. But whatever they found, nobody wanted Sarah to take to school. Nana didn't want her knitting taken.

Daddy said no about the red watering-can, because it was used for weedkiller. Mummy said she couldn't manage without her red slippers for even one day and everyone said the telephone couldn't go. Even Jam Samwidge hissed when Sarah tried to take off his red collar. When Sarah went to bed, she felt sad.

"I don't want to be the only one without a red thing."

In the morning, Sarah got dressed in her favourite red jumper, her new tartan skirt, her red socks and her wellington boots. Finally she put on the red wooden bracelet that Kathy gave her at her birthday party. But when it was time to go to school, she still didn't have anything to take to school for the Red Table.

"Pity about the front door," said Mummy as she bumped Lucy down the steps in her buggy.

As usual, Sarah said hello to the snapdragons in the front garden, who said hello back to her when she pressed the sides of their faces. Then she noticed what colour they were!

"Mummy, can I take some snapdragons for the Red Table?"

"Of course," said Mummy, and Sarah picked three crimson snapdragons.

"Take a tomato too," said Mummy, "not one that's still green or only orange."

Sarah chose a really ripe tomato and then Mummy reached up and picked a spray of scarlet berries from the tree.

So when Sarah got to school, she had three things for the Red Table and she took them straight to Miss Munro. The Red Table was already quite full. There was a red scarf, a bright red rainhat, a shiny red ball for a christmas tree, a pot of strawberry jam, an Indian headdress made of red feathers and a glass jar with one red rose in it. Jamie had brought a bright red chilli pepper.

Miss Munro put Sarah's snapdragons and berries in with the rose and put the tomato on the table.

"I hope no-one eats it," said Sarah.

"They'd better not try to eat the chilli!" said Jamie. "It would burn their mouths."

Miss Munro looked at Sarah in her red jumper, tartan skirt, socks and wellingtons.

"I see something else for our Red Table," she said. Sarah felt a bit worried. Was it her red bracelet? She was sure that Kathy wouldn't want her to take it off. But the next minute, Miss Munro had cleared a big space on the table and she lifted *Sarah* up and put her on it.

"Come and see our Red Table now!" said Miss Munro and all the children came to look at Sarah.

19

THREE

Sarah and the New Baby

Sarah's mummy was going to have another baby. Her tummy was getting very big and she got tired pushing Lucy to nursery in the buggy.

One evening Mummy was giving Sarah a bedtime cuddle. It was a bit difficult for Sarah to fit on Mummy's lap because there didn't seem to be much lap left.

"Do you remember when Lucy was born?" Mummy asked Sarah. Sarah shook her head. She was sucking her thumb and trying to curl up small enough to fit on Mummy's lap.

"Well, we were very lucky because Nana lives here all the time. So when Daddy had to take me to hospital it was all right because Nana was already here to look after you."

Sarah took her thumb out. "She forgot that I take the raisins out of my muesli before the milk goes on."

Her mummy laughed. "You see, you *do* remember. And then Daddy brought you and Nana to see Lucy and me in the hospital . . ."

"And I said she looked like a squashed tomato," said Sarah.

"That's right," said Mummy.

22

"Is Nana going to look after me *and* Lucy this time?" asked Sarah. "You must tell her about the raisins before you go to hospital."

Mummy gave Sarah a hug. "Don't worry, I'll remind her. But I might not need to. You see, this time, I'm going to have the baby at home. So I won't need to be away from you and Lucy even for one night. Of course I will be tired after the baby's born, so I will need Nana and Daddy to help with looking after you."

"I can help too," said Sarah. "I'm a big girl now."

"Yes, you are," said Mummy, "ever so much bigger than when Lucy was born. And the first thing you can help me do is get your bedroom ready."

The next morning a van came with a huge parcel. Mummy and Daddy unpacked it on the floor of Sarah and Lucy's bedroom. It was lots of bits of wood and two mattresses and a picture with instructions. Sarah guessed first.

"Bunk beds! Can I have the top one?"

"Yes you can," said Daddy, "but there's a long way to go before this lot looks anything like a bed. Can you take Lucy and play with her until we've got it set up?"

Sarah and Lucy played downstairs for a long time and then Lucy helped Nana make the

23

lunch. There was a lot of banging from upstairs and sometimes they heard shouting. Then Mummy and Daddy came down.

"Come and see," they said.

Sarah's old bed had gone. Daddy said he had put it in the loft. In its place was a pair of bunk beds with a ladder. Mummy and Sarah made up the top bunk and put all Sarah's toy animals at the end.

"You can sleep in it tonight," she said.

Lucy was going to sleep in the bottom one.

"What about Lucy's cot?" said Sarah.

"Aha!" said Daddy. "Who do you think is going to sleep in that?"

"My new sister," said Sarah.

But the cot had to go into Mummy and Daddy's room first because the new baby would need to be fed even in the night.

After lunch Daddy got down lots more things from the loft. Sarah remembered some of them. There was a carrycot and a set of wheels, a baby bath and a stand and a thing like a tiny frilly sleeping bag with handles.

"Oh dear," said Mummy, "everything looks very dusty. It will all have to be washed."

"There's all sorts of things up here, Sarah," said Daddy. "Do you want to come and see?"

So Sarah climbed carefully up the ladder

and Daddy lifted her into the loft.

"There's my bed!" said Sarah.

"Mm," said Daddy. "Your *old* bed. You've got a new one now. And there's your old high-chair and your old baby-bouncer."

"Am I going to have a new high-chair and a new baby-bouncer as well?" asked Sarah.

Daddy laughed. "No, just a new baby to put in the old ones. But she'll be too small for them just yet. So I'll leave them up here till we need them."

"Look," said Sarah, "there's my old toddle-truck. She can have that when she's bigger too."

Daddy and Sarah came down the ladder.

"A baby couldn't climb up in the loft, could she?" asked Sarah.

"No," said Daddy. "Even Lucy is a bit small to do that."

That night, Sarah got ready for bed early and climbed up the ladder into her new bunk bed. It was very high and strange and she felt a bit scared.

"Don't be frightened, Panda," she said. "I won't let you fall out."

Lucy was in the bottom bunk bed. She started to cry. "This bed's too big for me. I want my cot."

Sarah climbed down the ladder and got into

bed with Lucy. "Panda's a bit frightened too. The top bunk's too high up for him. He can stay here and keep you company."

Lucy stopped crying. "I don't want the new baby to have my cot."

"Well," said Sarah, "it was *my* cot first, you know. Then you had it. The baby's going to have my high-chair too, when it's a bit bigger."

"Don't you mind?" asked Lucy.

"Not really," said Sarah. "I like being a big girl. Big girls can go up ladders."

"Can I go up a ladder?" asked Lucy.

"I don't think you're supposed to," said Sarah.

The next morning Daddy found Sarah and Lucy and Panda all cuddled up fast asleep in the top bunk bed.

A few days later when Sarah came out of school, Daddy was waiting at the gate.

"Where's Mummy?" asked Sarah.

"She's busy," said Daddy. "She's so busy, I had to come home from work specially."

"Is she getting something ready for the baby?" asked Sarah on the way home.

"Not exactly," said Daddy. "She's getting the baby ready for us. Come on, we must hurry. I don't want to miss the baby being born."

When Sarah got home, there was a blue car
outside the house.

"That's the midwife's car," said Daddy.
"Mrs Samuels has come to look after Mummy

27

while she has the baby."

"Can I say hello to Mummy," said Sarah.

Lucy and Nana were having tea in the kitchen, but Sarah wanted to see Mummy. Daddy took her into the big bedroom. Mummy wasn't in bed. She was sitting in a chair. There was a lady in a blue uniform with her hand on Mummy's tummy. She was looking at her watch.

"It's half past three," said Sarah, who had just learned to tell the time.

The lady laughed. "Thank you. I'll put my watch right."

Mummy held her arms out to Sarah and gave her a big hug.

"Come and have tea with us," said Sarah.

Mummy said, "I can't come just now, darling. But perhaps you could bring me some tea in here."

So Sarah and Daddy made Mummy a cup of tea and then it was time for children's programmes on TV. As a special treat Lucy and Sarah watched them in Nana's bedroom. When programmes were over, Nana showed them her treasures. She opened her jewellery box and let Sarah and Lucy try on the necklaces and bracelets. Then she showed them her photograph album of when Daddy was a little boy.

"Who's that baby?" asked Lucy.

"That's Daddy," said Sarah. "He looks like a squashed tomato too."

Just then, they heard Daddy calling them. They all went into the bedroom. Mummy was sitting up in bed looking very tired: but she gave them a big smile. The lady in the blue uniform was holding something in her arms that made a noise like Jam Samwidge miaowing for his supper.

"Hello, my darlings," said Mummy, "meet your new brother."

"He looks just like you when you were a baby, Daddy," said Sarah.

"He sounds just like you too," said Nana.

"Why is she a boy?" said Lucy.

"I think it's because he wasn't born in the hospital," said Sarah.

Then they all had a turn at holding the baby.

"What's for supper," said Sarah, "I'm starving."

"Me too," said Mummy, "I've worked hard this afternoon."

"Right," said Daddy. "Take-aways all round."

And he took Sarah and Lucy with him, to buy fish and chips for them and an Indian take-away for the grown-ups.

They all had a picnic on the floor in Mummy and Daddy's room, but Mummy had a tray on her lap in bed. Mrs Samuels sat on the floor and had supper with them. In Lucy's old cot the new baby made happy little noises.

"He's trying to join in the party," said Mummy.

"That's because it's really his birthday party," said Sarah. "Happy Birthday, baby!"

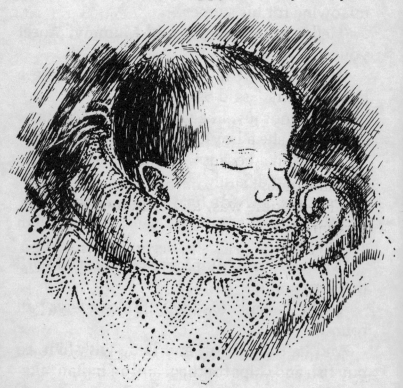

FOUR

Sarah finds a Name

"I'm a big sister twice now," said Sarah at breakfast. "Once to Lucy and once to . . . hey! What is our new baby's name?"

"He hasn't got one yet," said Daddy. "We were so sure we would have another girl that we didn't have a boy's name ready. Have you got any suggestions?"

Sarah thought hard. She was good at names. She had thought of Jam Samwidge for their cat. The trouble was, all her favourite names were girl's ones.

"If he was a girl," she began, "it would be easy. You could call him Mariette or Circlette or Anklette . . ."

"That's what your dolls are called," interrupted Lucy.

"I agree," said Daddy, "it would be very easy. There are lots of nice girls' names."

"You could call him after you," said Nana. "David is a very nice name."

"But it's too grown up for a baby," said Sarah. Everybody laughed.

"He needs a name to start off small, like him, and then stretch as he gets bigger, like a babygro," explained Sarah.

Daddy said, "You're quite right. I'll tell Mummy and it might help us to think of the right one. Now, you'll be late for school if you don't hurry. There's only one more week before the holidays."

At show and tell time, Sarah told everyone about the new baby and of course everyone wanted to know his name.

"He hasn't got one yet," said Sarah. "We're waiting for it to arrive."

"Let's have a competition!" said her friend Jamie. "Like the time we chose Woffle's name!"

Woffle was the class hamster and all the children had suggested a name for him and voted on the result.

"That's a good idea, Jamie," said Miss Munro. "Of course, Sarah's mummy and daddy might not choose any of the names we suggest. But it might help them to see the names you all think of."

32

So she got a cardboard box and lots of bits of paper and everyone had till the end of the day to write down a name for Sarah's baby brother.

Jamie wrote "Jamie" on his piece of paper, because it was his idea. Sarah didn't see what everybody else put but she was very excited when Daddy came to collect her. She wouldn't say what

was in the cardboard box till she got home.

"Hello, Lucy. Hello, Nana," she called. "I'm going to see Mummy and brother." She took the cardboard box into Mummy's bedroom. Mummy was giving the baby his milk in an armchair.

"Hello darling, what have you got there?"

"A name for the baby," said Sarah. "Lots of names – all the children in my class wrote one down."

"What a lovely idea," said Mummy. "Let me just finish giving him his milk and then we'll have tea and see what names are in the box."

So when the baby was asleep again, they all sat in the living room and pulled out names.

"What does this say?" asked Lucy, holding a piece of paper.

"Oh dear," said Nana. "It says, Woffle. We can't call him that."

Sarah giggled. "Let's put that one in the wastepaper basket. Now Nana, *you* try."

"Alexander," read out Nana.

"That's a nice one," said Mummy. "Let's make a pile of all the ones we like."

"Hm," said Daddy. "This is much more fun than just reading through a book of names. What's this one? Luke."

"That's much too like Lucy," said Sarah. "Let me try one."

Soon they had a small pile of names they

liked and the waste paper basket was full. The names they liked were:

Alexander
Robert
Daniel
and Tom

"Tom's the easiest to spell," said Sarah, "I don't know how to write Alexander. And it could be short for tomato, because he's red and wrinkly."

"Mm," said Mummy. "But it's really short for Thomas. And there do seem to be a lot of Toms around these days."

Daddy had a thought. "Did you write a name and put it in the box, Sarah?" he asked.

"No, I didn't even think of it," said Sarah. "But I will."

She asked Mummy for a bit of paper and wrote something down. Then she put it in the cardboard box.

Daddy unfolded it and read out, "Jack."

"I like that," said Mummy. "Why did you think of that?"

"It's short for Jack-in-the-box," said Sarah, "because he gave us all a surprise."

Everyone liked that idea. Nana was specially pleased. "My father was called Jack," she said.

The next afternoon after school, Daddy didn't take Sarah straight home. They went to

the Town Hall and sat down in a waiting room.

"What are we going to do here?" asked Sarah.

"Wait and see," said Daddy.

"Is this a waiting-and-seeing-room?" asked Sarah.

A lady came out of a door and asked them to come in. She had a desk and a lot of papers and pens.

"We've come to register a name for a new baby," said Daddy. "This is his big sister,

36

Sarah."

Then the lady wrote down what Daddy told her and he showed Sarah the piece of paper. It said, Jack Alexander David.

"Goody," said Sarah.

"But I shall call him Jack-in-the-box," said Daddy. "Because that's where we found his name."

FIVE

Sarah and the Supermarket

"Not instant porridge again, Sarah!" said Mummy.

"I like it," said Sarah, pouring herself a huge bowlful and adding milk and sugar. "Lots of people like it."

"For breakfast maybe, darling," said Daddy, "but not for tea. That's the third time you've had it today."

"What's wrong with it?" asked Sarah, stirring it up in her bowl.

"I always think it looks like polyfilla," said Nana. "I hope it tastes a bit better."

"Even polyfilla probably tastes nice if you mix as much milk and sugar with it as Sarah puts on that stuff," said Mummy.

"Can I see if it does?" asked Lucy.

"No!" said everybody.

Later on, when Sarah was playing in her

room and Daddy was bathing Jack, Mummy came in and said, "I'm worried about Sarah.

Ever since Jack was born, she's eaten hardly anything except instant porridge, fruit and the odd bit of cheese."

"Well," said Daddy, "that's quite a healthy diet, I shouldn't wonder."

"But it's a bit dull, isn't it? And it probably means she feels a bit annoyed with us for having another baby."

"Oh, you know Sarah. She gets some funny ideas but she always sorts herself out in the end," said Daddy, drying Jack on his lap.

"I know," said Mummy, "and I don't want to make a big scene about it in case it makes her even more fussy. But I do wish she'd eat what the rest of us are having."

"Well, let me have a word with her. "I'll take her shopping with me tomorrow night and we can have a chat then."

Before Jack was born, Daddy and Mummy used to go late-night shopping in the supermarket once a week, leaving Nana to babysit the girls. But Jack was very lively in the evenings and wouldn't drink milk from a bottle, so Mummy had to stay behind and Daddy usually did the shopping by himself now. But this week, he put Sarah in the car and they went together. In the supermarket, Sarah wanted to get in the trolley, even though she was really too big for it.

"This is fun, Daddy. What shall we buy first?"

"We come to all the breakfast cereals first," said Daddy.

"Don't forget to buy some more instant

porridge," said Sarah. "It's almost run out."

Daddy put two big boxes of the porridge into the trolley. Then he bought some butter and bacon.

"Come on Sarah," he said. "Get out of that trolley and suggest some things to buy. I'm running out of ideas."

So Sarah put some yoghurts in the trolley, and one packet of frankfurters and a big pizza. Then they came to the delicatessen counter and Daddy held her up to see all the interesting little cartons of olives and salads and the big cold sausages for slicing and the pies and cheeses. Sarah pointed to all sorts of things and the delicatessen lady weighed them and put them into little plastic boxes and then into paper bags and *then* stuck the price on them. She handed them to Sarah one at a time and she put them all in the trolley. It took Daddy and Sarah a long time to go round the supermarket and they were almost the last people to go through the checkout. Then they had to take everything to the car, so it was quite late when they got home. Lucy was already in bed. Nana was watching TV and Mummy was in the kitchen walking Jack up and down.

"Goodness!" she said, when she saw all the

bags. "What *have* you bought?"

"Give that young man to me for a bit," said Daddy, "and Sarah can explain the shopping to you while you unpack it."

Mummy's eyes grew bigger and bigger as she put away all the things they had bought. When Sarah had gone to bed, she said to Daddy, "You must have spent a fortune!"

"Well, a bit more than usual," said Daddy. "But wait and see. I think it may be worth it."

Next morning, when the others were having breakfast, Sarah went to the fridge and the cupboards and organised her own. This is what she put in her place:

        1 strawberry yoghurt
        2 crackers with cheese
        1 banana
        3 cherry tomatoes
        1 slice of garlic sausage

And she ate the lot. Her family stared in astonishment.

"Well!" said Nana at last, "that beats porridge for tea."

"I chose all these things at the supermarket," said Sarah proudly. "It was lovely and I'm going with Daddy every week."

"Aren't you going to eat polyfilla anymore?" asked Lucy.

"Well, sometimes, maybe . . ." said Sarah.

"I hope so," said Daddy. "We bought two big boxes of the stuff last night."

"Well, it will be very useful when Jack starts eating proper food, won't it, Mummy?" said Sarah. "It will be nice and sloppy for him. It's baby's food really."

"Yes, well, he certainly won't be able to eat a breakfast like yours for a long time," said Mummy.

"And when he gets hungry in the evening, Nana can mix him a bowl of it, so you'll be able to come shopping with Daddy and me. Won't that be good?"

"Yes," said Mummy, "I think instant porridge is going to be very useful, after all."

SIX

Sarah has
a Friend
to Play

Sarah was bored. Daddy had taken Lucy to a birthday party of one of her nursery school friends. Nana was out too, having tea with one of *her* friends. Mummy wouldn't play with her because she had too many jobs to do.

"Poor Sarah," said Mummy, "would you like to ask a friend round to play for the afternoon? I'll ring up Kathy's mummy if you like."

Kathy lived quite nearby and soon she was in Sarah's room all ready to play.

"What shall we do?" said Sarah.

"Let's play with your hospital set," said Kathy.

"OK," said Sarah. She loved playing hospitals and bandaging people up and pretending to give them injections. She had a real syringe (without the needle) that the vet had given her the last time they took Jam Samwidge to see him. But Kathy didn't want to be bandaged up and injected – she wanted to be the doctor herself.

"What about Noah's ark then?" said Kathy, when they couldn't agree.

"All right," said Sarah and they pulled out the wooden ark and got the old ice-cream box full of animals.

"I'm having the lions, the tigers, the elephants, the pandas, the giraffes, the zebras and the hippos," said Sarah.

"What can I have then?" asked Kathy.

"You can have the ostriches, the anteaters, the camels, the warthogs and the mooses," said Sarah.

"Well, I don't like those," said Kathy. "I'm not playing."

"Oh," said Sarah. "Shall we play with the doll's house?"

When Sarah's mummy came up to call them for tea, Kathy was playing with the doll's house and Sarah was playing with the ark.

After Kathy had gone home, Sarah's mummy said, "Did you like having Kathy to play, Sarah?"

"Not much," said Sarah. "She wanted all my best toys and she wanted to be the doctor."

'But you like being the doctor, don't you?"
said Mummy.

"Yes," said Sarah, "she wouldn't let me
bandage her up."

"Perhaps she would have if you'd let her
bandage you first," said Mummy. "You could
take turns to be the doctor. After all, it's more
fun playing hospitals with another person than
putting bandages on teddies and trying to give
poor old Jam Samwidge an injection."

"Hmm," said Sarah.

48

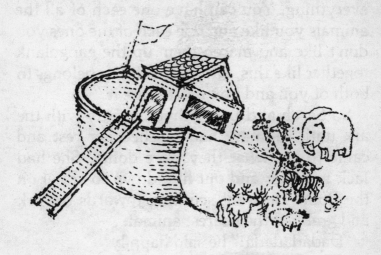

Next day she was playing Noah's ark with Lucy. Lucy started crying very loudly and Daddy came to see what was the matter.

"What's all this noise? Mummy's trying to have a little rest. Jack got her up three times in the night."

"Sarah *always* has the zebras and the nice animals," sobbed Lucy, "and I have to have the anteaters and ostriches and things and I don't like them."

"I don't like them either," said Sarah crossly.

"But the whole point about Noah's ark," said Daddy, "is that there are *two* of everything. You can have one each of all the animals you like and one each of the ones you don't like and march them up the gangplank together like this. After all, this toy belongs to both of you and you must share it."

So Sarah and Lucy played quietly with the ark until Mummy had finished her rest and came to see what they were doing. She had Jack with her and put him down to crawl on the floor. He went scuttling towards the ark and grabbed the nearest animal.

"Dadadadada!" he said happily.

"Oh dear," said Sarah, "we've only just worked out how to play with it with two people. It's a pity Noah didn't take *three* of everything."

That night Nana said, "There are lots of games that are much better with two or even three people. You and Lucy could play this one right now."

Nana showed them a box full of red and black wooden circles. She tipped the circles out and spread the box upside down, so that it made a little board covered in squares.

"I'm going to teach you how to play draughts," said Nana. And she did.

Next day, Sarah took her doctor's set to school. At playtime she found Kathy.

"Come on Kathy," she said, "let's play hospitals. We'll take turn at being the doctor and you can be first."

"OK," said Kathy. "Where does it hurt?"

"All over," said Sarah.

"Goodee," said Kathy and started to unroll the bandages.

SEVEN

Sarah and the Holiday House

Mummy and Daddy were packing to go on holiday. Sarah and Lucy were packing too. The only people who weren't packing were Jack, who was asleep, and Nana, who was staying behind to mind the house and feed Jam Samwidge. She was going on holiday later with her special friend.

Lucy's packing was soon done. She had a very small suitcase and she put in it her bucket and spade and her favourite teddy bear. Sarah's was taking longer. She had a proper case all to herself and was supposed to put sensible things like nighties and socks in it, but she kept thinking of more toys she might need. Several times Jam Samwidge packed himself, which didn't help. He hated it when the family went on holiday.

Next morning they were all ready to go and piled themselves and all their baggage into the car.

"I wish Nana was coming with us," said Sarah, as

they waved goodbye to her from the car windows.

"My dear Sarah," said Daddy, "where on earth would we put her, or her luggage, in this squash?"

"*I* wish Jam Samwidge was coming," said Lucy.

"He'd hate it," said Mummy. "You know how he likes his own house and garden and his own things."

"So do I," said Sarah.

Daddy laughed. "I hope you're not going to be homesick before we've even left our street!"

A long time later, they arrived in a little seaside town and stopped outside a small white house with a green door. Lucy was fast asleep in her car-seat. While Daddy was getting Jack's carrycot out of the car, Sarah rushed up the garden path with Mummy, who found the key under a flower-pot and let them in. Downstairs had a living-room, a kitchen and a bathroom.

"How funny to have the bathroom downstairs," said Sarah. "It's an upside down house."

"Well I'm glad they didn't put the kitchen up those steep and windy stairs," said Mummy.

"Can I go up and explore?" said Sarah.

"Yes," said Mummy. "You can do that while Daddy and I unpack."

Up the narrow staircase, which had a rope to hang on to instead of bannisters, there was a room on the right with a double bed and a cot. On the left was a smaller room with one single bed. The roofs were slopey and the rooms had odd little corners. It was a very old house.

"Mummy!" shouted Sarah down the stairs. "There aren't enough beds! I can't sleep with Lucy in a single bed."

"Hang on," called Mummy. "I'm coming up."

When Mummy came upstairs, she took Sarah into the big bedroom and opened a door which Sarah had thought was a cupboard. It led into a little room with one bed, a chest-of-drawers, a bookcase and a window that looked out on to the sea.

"There," said Mummy. "You've got the only room with a sea-view!"

"You mean this secret little room is for me?" said Sarah.

"Yes, darling. Lucy can have the other one. That is, if you like it."

"Yippee!" said Sarah and rushed down the stairs to get her suitcase.

When Mummy and Daddy had made all the beds and cooked the first supper in the holiday house, it was time for Lucy and Jack to go to bed.

"Can we go to the sea?" asked Lucy.

"Tomorrow morning," promised Daddy.

Sarah stayed up a bit later and wrote a

postcard to Nana. She had brought it with her specially in her suitcase – it had a picture of a big red London bus. Sarah wrote:

Dear Nana
Are house is ace
i have got a secert
room and I can seqe
the seqa.
I miss you a Lot. PLeS
give Jam Samwidge a
big x from me.
Love form
Sarah xx♡xx

In the morning, Sarah woke up early and pulled back her curtains. The sun was shining and already the sea was sparkling and glittering. Sarah went back to bed and thought about Mummy and Daddy and Jack all asleep next door and wondered if it was too early to get up. Presently she heard Jack cry and then heard the stairs creak as Daddy went downstairs to make Mummy a cup of tea. Sarah opened her door and saw Mummy feeding Jack in bed. She snuggled in beside her in the warm place where Daddy had been.

"Hello, holiday girl," said Mummy. "How did you sleep in your little shoe-box of a room?"

"Lovely," said Sarah, "I think it's a jewel-box and I'm going to fill it up with treasures."

"Do you think this is going to be a good holiday?" asked Mummy.

"The best," said Sarah, "because you are the best mummy in the world and Jack is the best baby brother."

"What about me?" said Daddy, coming in with two mugs of tea, and Sarah gave him such a big hug he nearly spilt it.

EIGHT

Sarah and the Tooth

When the summer holidays were over and Sarah went back to school, she had a new teacher – Mrs Ray. Lucy was still in the nursery and Jack was nearly six months old. He could sit up and eat porridge and he could giggle and chuckle.

But not long after Sarah's next birthday, Jack stopped giggling and chuckling and went back to crying and howling. Sarah was learning to write at school. She drew a picture of a baby with a big round mouth like a cave. Underneath it she wrote:

my brother Jack
keeps us all awayk

Mrs Ray showed her how to spell "awake" properly. While Mrs Ray talked to her about her picture, Sarah fiddled with one of her bottom teeth.

"Oh!" she said. "It wobbles."

"Let's have a look," said Mrs Ray. "Oh yes, you're going to lose that soon. Don't forget to put it under your pillow for the tooth fairy."

Sarah wiggled and wobbled that tooth for over a week. Mrs Ray got quite fed up with the sight of it. So did Lucy and Mummy and Daddy and Nana. The only ones who didn't mind were Jam Samwidge and Jack. The cat just opened his mouth wide and yawned to show Sarah all his perfect sharp white teeth. Jack smiled and showed his gums, before going back to howling again.

Children's teeth were dropping out left, right

and centre at school. Some lost theirs, others said the tooth fairy had left them 50p. When Sarah told Daddy this he said they must have a very rich fairy in their street, but he thought the one who came to the house with the red door would only manage 10p for a tooth.

"Mind you, it has to be a nice white one with no holes in it," he said, "otherwise she won't give a button for it."

One day after school Sarah was playing with Jack while Mummy made the supper. He was much more like his old self – cooing and gurgling at her. (Sarah and Jam Samwidge were his favourite people for smiling at.) Sarah bent down and tickled him in the tummy and he gave a fat, rich chuckle. Then Sarah saw he had a very small white tooth sticking up at the bottom of his smile.

"Mummy, Mummy," she shouted and ran out of the room just as Nana was coming in with a tea tray.

"Careful!" said Nana, but too late. Sarah had bumped her mouth on the tray and made it bleed. She started crying and Mummy came in.

"Whatever is it now?" asked Mummy, but she stopped being cross when she saw the blood. She dabbed Sarah's mouth with a tissue then said "Oh!"

"What is it?"said Sarah, who was scared of blood.

"Your tooth, it's gone," said Mummy. "We

must look for it on the floor."

Sarah stopped crying and started to laugh. "When I bumped my mouth I was coming to tell you about *Jack's* tooth."

"Jack's tooth?" said Mummy. "He hasn't got any yet."

"Oh yes he has," said Sarah. "Look!"

And she tickled him again, so Nana and Mummy could see.

Then Lucy came in and she had to show her too. And all over again when Daddy came home. As for Sarah's tooth, they could not find it, till they saw Jam Samwidge batting something hard around the floor and trying to throw it up and catch it. He was quite cross when they took the tooth away from him, so Nana gave him an empty cotton-reel to play with instead. Sarah washed the tooth and wrapped it in cotton-wool and put it under her pillow. Mummy put her to bed that night. They had to whisper because Lucy was asleep.

'Do you think the tooth fairy will come?' asked Sarah.

"Oh I think the tooth fairy has been very busy round this house today," said Mummy, 'I think she's sure to come." She gave Sarah a kiss.

"Do you know, I can remember when that tooth of yours came."

"Just like Jack's?" asked Sarah.

"Just like Jack's," said Mummy.

"And was I just as cross as Jack before it came?"

"Just as cross."

"Jack's a very sweet baby, isn't he?" said Sarah. "Was I as nice as him?"

"Just as nice," said Mummy. "But do you know what?"

"What?" asked Sarah, snuggling down in her top bunk bed with her panda.

"I think you're even nicer as you are now," said Mummy.

"Mmm," said Sarah sleepily. "Big girls are best . . ."